A Cretaceous Adventure

# Dinosaur Cove™

## Flight of the
## Winged Serpent

by
REX STONE

illustrated by
MIKE SPOOR

Series created by
Working Partners Ltd

OXFORD
UNIVERSITY PRESS

Special thanks to Jan Burchett and Sara Vogler

Especially for Theo and Ben Wheadon, with love

# OXFORD
UNIVERSITY PRESS

Great Clarendon Street, Oxford OX2 6DP
Oxford University Press is a department of the University of Oxford.
It furthers the University's objective of excellence in research, scholarship,
and education by publishing worldwide in

Oxford   New York

Auckland   Cape Town   Dar es Salaam   Hong Kong   Karachi
Kuala Lumpur   Madrid   Melbourne   Mexico City   Nairobi
New Delhi   Shanghai   Taipei   Toronto

With offices in

Argentina   Austria   Brazil   Chile   Czech Republic   France   Greece
Guatemala   Hungary   Italy   Japan   Poland   Portugal   Singapore
South Korea   Switzerland   Thailand   Turkey   Ukraine   Vietnam

Oxford is a registered trade mark of Oxford University Press
in the UK and in certain other countries

First published 2008
First published in this edition 2013

British Library Cataloguing in Publication Data

Data available

ISBN: 978-0-19-273933-9

1 3 5 7 9 10 8 6 4 2

Printed in India by Thomson Press India Ltd.

Paper used in the production of this book is a natural,
recyclable product made from wood grown in sustainable forests
The manufacturing process conforms to the environmental
regulations of the country of origin

# Dinosaur Cove™

# FACT FILE

➭ JAMIE HAS JUST MOVED FROM THE CITY TO LIVE IN THE LIGHTHOUSE IN DINOSAUR COVE. JAMIE'S DAD IS OPENING A DINOSAUR MUSEUM ON THE BOTTOM FLOOR OF THE LIGHTHOUSE. WHEN JAMIE GOES HUNTING FOR FOSSILS IN THE CRUMBLING CLIFFS ON THE BEACH HE MEETS A LOCAL BOY, TOM, AND THE TWO DISCOVER AN AMAZING SECRET: A WORLD WITH **REAL, LIVE DINOSAURS!** WALKING ON THE GROUND WITH THE DINOSAURS IS ONE THING, BUT FLYING IN THE AIR WITH THEM IS A DIFFERENT MATTER!

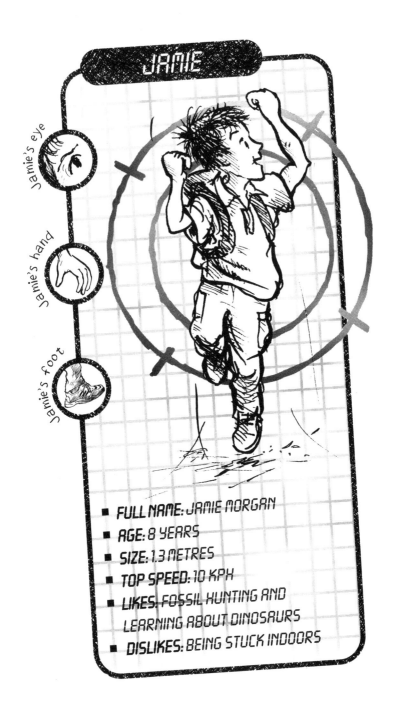

# JAMIE

Jamie's eye

Jamie's hand

Jamie's foot

- **FULL NAME:** JAMIE MORGAN
- **AGE:** 8 YEARS
- **SIZE:** 1.3 METRES
- **TOP SPEED:** 10 KPH
- **LIKES:** FOSSIL HUNTING AND LEARNING ABOUT DINOSAURS
- **DISLIKES:** BEING STUCK INDOORS

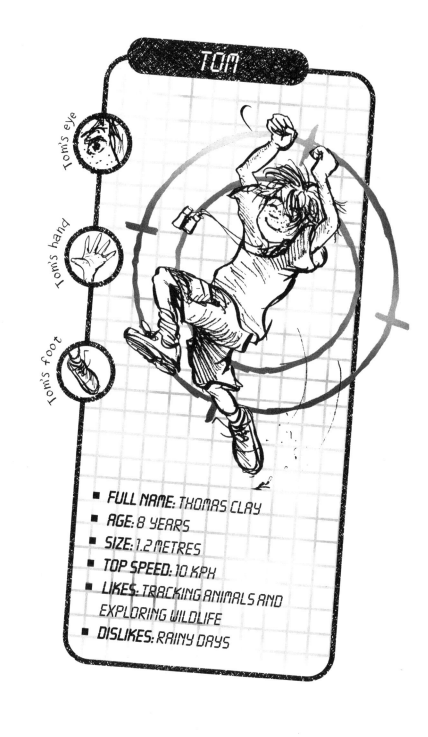

TOM

Tom's eye

Tom's hand

Tom's foot

- **FULL NAME:** THOMAS CLAY
- **AGE:** 8 YEARS
- **SIZE:** 1.2 METRES
- **TOP SPEED:** 10 KPH
- **LIKES:** TRACKING ANIMALS AND EXPLORING WILDLIFE
- **DISLIKES:** RAINY DAYS

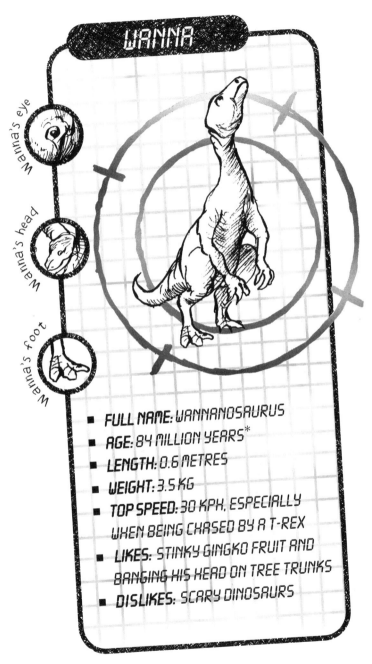

## WANNA

Wanna's eye

Wanna's head

Wanna's foot

- **FULL NAME:** WANNANOSAURUS
- **AGE:** 84 MILLION YEARS*
- **LENGTH:** 0.6 METRES
- **WEIGHT:** 3.5 KG
- **TOP SPEED:** 30 KPH, ESPECIALLY WHEN BEING CHASED BY A T-REX
- **LIKES:** STINKY GINGKO FRUIT AND BANGING HIS HEAD ON TREE TRUNKS
- **DISLIKES:** SCARY DINOSAURS

*****NOTE:** SCIENTISTS CALL THIS PERIOD THE LATE CRETACEOUS

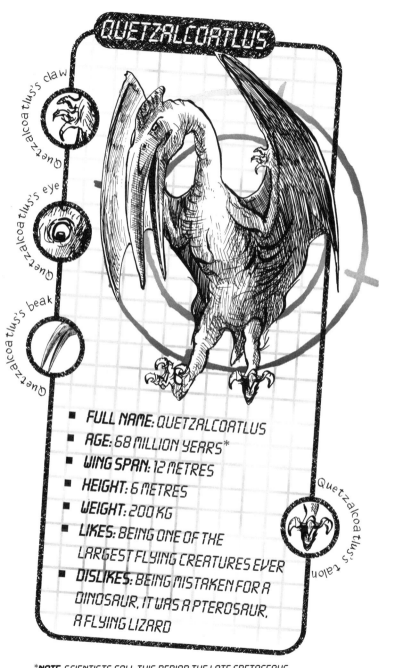

## QUETZALCOATLUS

Quetzalcoatlus's claw

Quetzalcoatlus's eye

Quetzalcoatlus's beak

Quetzalcoatlus's talon

- **FULL NAME:** QUETZALCOATLUS
- **AGE:** 68 MILLION YEARS*
- **WING SPAN:** 12 METRES
- **HEIGHT:** 6 METRES
- **WEIGHT:** 200 KG
- **LIKES:** BEING ONE OF THE LARGEST FLYING CREATURES EVER
- **DISLIKES:** BEING MISTAKEN FOR A DINOSAUR, IT WAS A PTEROSAUR, A FLYING LIZARD

*NOTE: SCIENTISTS CALL THIS PERIOD THE LATE CRETACEOUS

DINOSAUR COVE

Village

Marina

Sealight Head

10

Landslips where
clay and fossils are

Muddy beach

DINO CAVE

High Tide beach line

Low tide beach line

Sea

Smuggler's Point

CHAPTER 1

'This exhibit looks so cool!' exclaimed Jamie, as his best friend Tom glued on the last miniature jungle tree.

The two boys had spent the morning painting the prehistoric

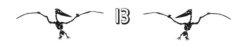

landscape and were just finishing the scenery. The scale model was as big as the table top and was going to be one of the exhibits in Jamie's dad's new dinosaur museum on the bottom floor of the old lighthouse where they lived.

'The marsh is my favourite,' Tom said, putting down the glue.

The model was labelled 'Late Cretaceous Period' and had a jungle, a plain, a beach with cliffs, and an eerie-looking marsh. Dad had set up a smoke machine under the table so that smoke blew over the marsh like mist.

Dad walked into the room with the post. 'You two

have done a brilliant job painting the ocean,' he told them, and grinned at their paint-splattered clothes. 'And yourselves!'

Next, Jamie and Tom added the most important items to the display—the dinosaurs! They arranged a herd of triceratops on the green plain.

'They're just right there,' said Dad. 'They look as if they're grazing.' He stuck his head into a crate and started rummaging. Sawdust flew everywhere. 'Can't find the edmontosaurus,' came his muffled voice. 'I'm sure they're in here somewhere.'

'Dad's models are great,' whispered Jamie, 'but they're not as good as the real thing.'

Jamie and Tom had a secret. They had discovered the entrance to an amazing land of living dinosaurs, and they visited it whenever they could.

Jamie picked up a tyrannosaurus rex and made it run across the plain towards an ankylosaurus with a roar.

Tom snatched up the ankylosaurus. 'Not such an easy meal, you bully!' He swung the tiny anky's clubbed tail at the t-rex.

'Whoops!' Tom gasped as the t-rex went flying out of Jamie's hand towards a shelf full of model creatures.

*WHACK!*

The t-rex crashed into a large winged creature which wobbled and fell.

Jamie dived like a goalie and caught it before it hit the floor.

'Good catch!' gasped Tom.

Jamie's dad came running over.

'Sorry, Mr Morgan,' said Tom. 'Is it broken?'

Jamie's dad checked the model's wings. 'No damage done,' he told them. 'Now, where should this go on the display?'

Jamie looked at the long beak, the outstretched wings, and bony crest on the head. 'It's a sort of pterosaur, isn't it?'

'Yes, it's a quetzalcoatlus. Here's its label.'

'*Ket-sal-kow-at-lus*,' Jamie read. 'That's a mouthful.'

'One of the biggest flying reptiles,' Dad explained. 'It had a twelve metre wingspan.'

'That's more than six Dads lying head to toe.' Jamie flung his arms out wide.

'What a monster!' Tom said.

'One thing we don't know is where these quetzies nested,' said Dad. 'On the marsh, on the beach, or in the jungle.' He put the quetzy back on the shelf. 'Here's a quest for you, boys. Do some research and help me decide where on the model to put it. That'll keep you out of trouble.'

Jamie and Tom grinned at each other. They knew exactly where to find out where the quetzalcoatlus nested—Dino World!

Jamie scooped up his backpack and charged after Tom down the rocky

steps from the lighthouse.
They raced across the
pebbly beach, whooping
with excitement, to the
steep headland path.

Clambering over the
mossy boulders they
were soon at the old
smugglers' cave—and
the entrance to their
secret world.

Tom slipped inside
with Jamie close behind.
They squeezed through
the tiny opening to
the second chamber.
Jamie shone his torch
over the rock floor.

'Here are the
footprints,' he said.
'Let's go!'

One step at a time, Jamie and
Tom followed the fossilized dinosaur
tracks that led to the wall at the back
of the cave. One . . . two . . . The
familiar crack of light appeared in
the wall . . . three . . . four . . . The
crack widened . . . Five!

When Jamie opened his eyes, the
ground was spongy under his feet.
Jamie and Tom were in Dino World
again!

**CHAPTER 2**

Jamie stepped out of the cave and
squinted in the bright sunlight.
He breathed in the hot, damp air.
'Awesome!'

A bristly tongue licked his hand. A
little dinosaur with greenish brown

markings stood looking up hopefully at him.

'It's Wanna!' he cried.

Tom gave the wannanosaurus a welcoming pat on his hard, flat head. Wanna wagged his tail happily and stuck out his tongue to investigate a blue spot on Jamie's shorts.

*Grunk!* Wanna spat.

'Paint tastes horrible, doesn't it, Wanna?' said Jamie. 'Let's find you some nice, stinky gingkoes to make it better.' He reached up and picked a handful of sticky orange fruits from a nearby gingko tree.

Wanna gulped down the gingkoes in one go, juice spilling out of his mouth and down his chest. His long, bristly tongue licked his face and he grunked happily.

Jamie stuck a few more gingkoes in his backpack.

The boys went to the edge of the steep slope that led down to the jungle. They scanned the thick green canopy of trees below.

'One thing's for sure,' said Tom, 'quetzies couldn't live in there—not with that huge wingspan. The trees are too close together. And I don't see any nests in the tree tops.'

Jamie opened his Fossil Finder and put quetzalcoatlus in the search.

'*THOUGHT TO HAVE EATEN LIKE HERON, DIVING DOWN FOR FISH,*' he read. 'So maybe they live near water.'

'Misty Lagoon?' said Tom. 'But I only remember seeing

smaller pterosaurs there—nothing as big as a quetzy.'

'How about White Ocean?' said Jamie eagerly. He shielded his eyes with his hand and peered out over the jungle, to where the ocean waves broke in a white line.

Tom whipped his compass out of his pocket. 'West it is.'

The boys made their way

down into the thick, damp
undergrowth of the jungle.
Wanna ran happily alongside
them. He stopped to headbutt a
pine tree and greedily ate the
cones that fell. The shower of
cones disturbed a host of
brightly coloured butterflies as
big as the boys' hands. They
swarmed for a moment and
then settled on a bush
covered in white flowers.

The boys crossed the
river and gradually
the dense jungle
thinned.

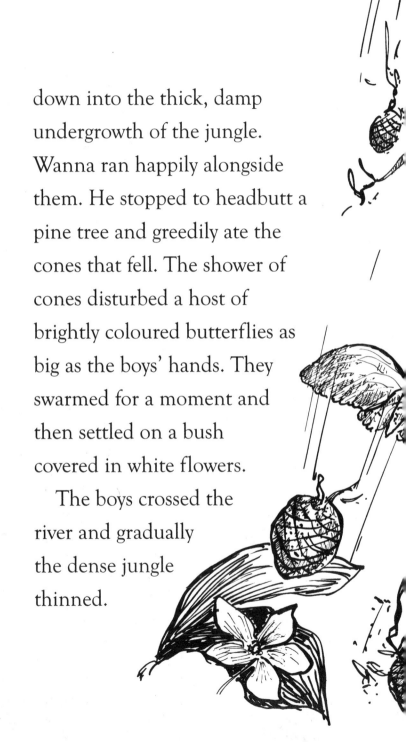

They passed the
lagoon and the
ground became
sandy, with tall,
spiky plants
shooting up in
places.

'I can hear waves
breaking,' exclaimed
Tom. 'Race you!'

They charged through
the last few trees and out into
the sunlight.

'Wow!' breathed Jamie,
skidding to a halt. He pointed
down the beach. 'Check out

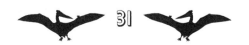

31

those cliffs. They're even higher than back in Dinosaur Cove.'

Sharp ledges and leafy green bushes covered the huge cliff-face. In front of them, the golden beach stretched towards the water. Wanna

sniffed around, getting his snout covered in sand.

'Maybe this is his first trip to the seaside.' Jamie laughed. 'Sorry we forgot the bucket and spade, Wanna.'

'Awesome!' shouted Tom above the sound of the crashing breakers and the gusting wind. 'Look at those waves. Fantastic for surfing.'

'If you don't mind the predators,' Jamie reminded him. 'I bet it's not just lobsters and crabs under there.'

He typed *LATE CRETACEOUS SEA CREATURES* into the Fossil Finder and scrolled down the entries.

'*ELASMOSAURUS: HUGE, LONG- NECKED, MARINE*

*REPTILE*. Looks like the Loch Ness Monster.' He showed Tom the picture on the screen. *'PLATECARPUS: SHARP-TOOTHED SEA LIZARD*. There are sharks, too.'

'I could do a great TV commentary from my surfboard.' Tom pretended to be riding the waves and speaking into a microphone. 'Here we have the gigantic platecarpus. I can see every one of this sea lizard's jagged teeth and . . . Aaaaagh, it's got me!'

Jamie laughed as his friend fell on the sand and fought an invisible platecarpus.

Suddenly Tom
jumped to his feet.
'What's that?' He pointed
out to the horizon. 'It's the size
of a plane.'

Jamie screened his eyes with his
hand. Far away over the sea, a huge
winged creature was gliding in large
graceful circles, rising and falling
with the air currents.

Tom whistled. 'It's just
like your dad's model.

And look, here come some more.'
    The two boys looked at each other.
    'It's a quetzalcoatlus!' they
shouted.

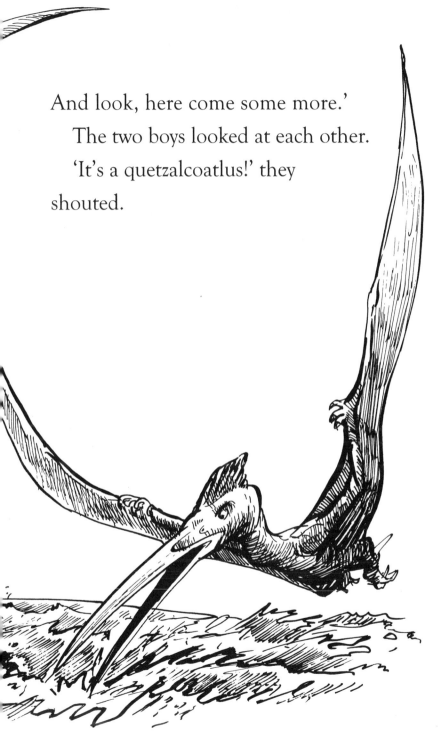

## CHAPTER 3

Jamie and Tom watched as the huge quetzies made lazy circles above the surf. One of them was getting closer.

'It's searching for fish,' said Tom. 'Do you think its nest is nearby?'

'It might be in the sand,' suggested Jamie. 'Like a turtle's.'

They walked along the high tide line, crunching through fragments of patterned baculite shell, but couldn't see any imprints or patterns in the ground to suggest a nest.

'Wouldn't this look good in your dad's museum?' Tom said, picking up a shell. 'Shame it would just turn to dust if we took it back.'

'Even if we could,' added Jamie, 'these have been extinct for millions of years. Dad would want to know how we found one that's not a fossil.'

Wanna trotted down the beach and looked suspiciously at the waves.

'Going for a paddle, Wanna?' called Tom.

The little dinosaur crept towards the edge of the water and stuck in his snout.

*Grunk!*

He spluttered and darted back.
The boys burst out laughing.

'The salt must taste worse than
paint,' said Jamie. 'Poor Wanna.'

Wanna scratched at his mouth
with his front claws as if he was
trying to get rid of the taste.

Then Tom spotted a cave at the
bottom of the cliffs. 'That would be a
great hiding place for the quetzy's nest.'

The boys went to investigate. Jamie
pulled out his torch and shone it into
the dark beyond the cave entrance
but it was empty. There was no sign
of a quetzy nest.

# AAAA*RK!*

The boys whirled round at the deafening sound behind them. An enormous shadow was moving over the sand. They dived into the cave mouth. Wanna grunked in alarm and followed.

A gigantic creature swept down and landed on the sand with a loud flapping of wings that sounded like boat sails in the wind. Jamie and Tom stared in amazement. In front of them were two long scaly legs with massive clawed feet. As they looked up they could see a featherless body

and neck that seemed to snake up to the sky. It stood above them, as tall as a house, twisting its long neck slowly this way and that. Then it opened its beak and gave out a loud *AAAARK!*

'It's the quetzy,' breathed Tom.

'That's one weird reptile,' said Jamie in amazement. 'Like a fold-up paper aeroplane with skin for wings.'

The huge pterosaur began to clump awkwardly across the sand, head forward, using the claws on its wings as front feet.

'Bats walk like that,' said Tom. 'I've seen it on a wildlife programme.'

A gust of wind buffeted the quetzy. It ran a few steps on its long skinny legs, caught the updraught and took off.

'See where it goes!' cried Jamie.

The boys dashed out from the shelter of the cave mouth and watched the quetzalcoatlus rise. The wind buffeted it back towards the cliffs, but soon it turned and soared, flapping its powerful wings to gain height. It circled around the cliff top and descended, feet out for landing. At last, with a loud *AAARK*, it disappeared from view.

'I bet its nest is up *there*,' said Jamie. 'We have to get to the top.'

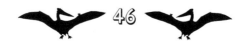

'It'll be a
tough climb,' said
Tom, squinting up at
the cliff-face. 'But we
can do it. There are
indents for our feet.'

'And we can use
the bushes to cling to,'
agreed Jamie.

SQUAWK!

Something landed on
the sand behind them.
It lay on its back with its
skinny feet in the air. It
looked like a large,
featherless chicken.

'Where did that come from?'
exclaimed Tom, staring up at the cliffs.

'I don't know,' gasped Jamie.
'Watch out!'

They darted back as a second
one fell out of the sky and plopped
down on to the sand. 'They must
be coming from up there,'
Tom said.

A third creature appeared over the
top of the cliffs. It flapped its wings
desperately and then cartwheeled
down, squawking, to land right in
front of them.

'They've got crests.' Tom pointed
to the little bony lump on top of each

head. 'Long beaks, claws on their wings . . . '

'They're baby quetzies!'

The boys watched as the three young reptiles struggled to their feet and waddled up and down flapping their wings.

'They're trying to take off,' said Tom.

'They look like big wind-up toys.' Jamie grinned at the funny sight.

*Grunk, grunk!*

Wanna scuttled up to the gawky creatures. The baby quetzies peered down at him and squawked happily. 'What is it, boy?' asked Jamie. 'Are you saying hello?'

*Grunk!*

Wanna nudged the nearest chick with his nose, then darted out of reach. The little quetzies clumped after him on all fours, squeaking with delight. Wanna stopped, waggled his tail at them and dashed off down the beach. His new playmates followed.

Tom chuckled. 'They're playing tag. Let's get a closer look.'

As soon as they saw the boys coming, the baby quetzies left Wanna and waddled towards them.

'They're not scared of us,' said Tom. 'They look really friendly.'

'Whoa!' Jamie backed off as a long pointed beak was pushed in his face, and another pecked at his trainers. 'A bit too friendly.'

*AARK!* The boys looked up. The mother quetzy was gliding in circles, looking down angrily, blocking out the sun.

'Run!' shouted Jamie.

Jamie and Tom flattened themselves against the cliff-face, but Wanna hadn't noticed the danger. He ran round the babies, grunking and nudging them to play again.

'Wanna's in danger,' said Tom. 'The mother might attack him!'

'Come here, Wanna,' Jamie shouted but the little quetzies were making so much noise that Wanna didn't hear him.

The huge quetzalcoatlus began to descend, stretching out long, sharp claws as she came.

AAARK!

'We've got to save Wanna!' yelled Jamie, darting forwards.

'It's too late.' Tom pulled his friend back. 'There's nothing we can do.'

Swoosh! The boys felt the rush of air as the giant pterosaur swooped down over the sand. A second later she was making for the sky.

The babies were gone—and so was Wanna!

CHAPTER 4

Jamie and Tom stared open-mouthed as the quetzalcoatlus rose in the air. Wanna and the three chicks were dangling from her claws. They could see the little dinosaur's tail waggling with fright.

Jamie shook Tom's arm. 'We've got to get up those cliffs,' he urged. 'We must rescue Wanna.'

'Too right,' said Tom. 'Before he's turned into quetzy food!'

They began to climb, side by side. It was a slow job. The cliff footholds were very small and the pale rock crumbled under their trainers and showered down. Gradually they edged their way up.

'What's that?' Jamie asked, looking at something jutting out above them.

'Looks like a ledge of rock,' Tom said. 'It sticks out quite far. And we've got to get over it.'

Luckily the ledge was covered in creepers.

Jamie gave one a tug. It held firm. 'There's only one thing for it,' he said.

'OK, boss,' grinned Tom.

Gripping tightly with his hands and hooking his feet over the creepers, Jamie hung upside down underneath the ledge. He made his way like a spider on a ceiling to the edge of the overhang. He scrabbled with his fingers to find a handhold on the top of the ledge.

Suddenly he lost his grip and found himself hanging by his trainers. It was like dangling from a

giant climbing frame—a
climbing frame with a deadly
drop beneath it.

'Jamie!' yelled Tom in alarm.

'I'm OK,' Jamie shouted back.
He swung his arms up as hard as he
could and on the third attempt
managed to grab the foliage again.
He waited until he'd got his breath
back, then, tensing every muscle, he
heaved himself onto the top of the
ledge.

Soon Tom's hand appeared.
Jamie took him firmly by the wrist

and helped him up.
The boys saw that the
top of the ledge was also
covered by a spongy bed
of creepers.

'Awesome!' breathed
Tom. 'We did it.'

'And there's the top
of the cliffs,' cried
Jamie, pointing a little
way above their heads.
'Wanna, here we come!'

They scrambled up to the cliff
edge and looked over. It was nothing
like the cliffs back home, which were
covered in grass and wild flowers.

Here there was bare rock with a few scattered prickly plants sticking up. The mother quetzy sat a little way from them.

'There's no sign of Wanna,' said Jamie, 'or the babies.'

'Let's get behind that bush with the red flowers,' whispered Tom. 'The quetzy won't be able to see us there.'

Jamie and Tom crawled commando style to the thick bush.

Jamie carefully parted some leaves.
The mother quetzy filled his view.

'The nest must be somewhere close
by,' he told Tom. 'But it's hard to
spot it with that huge pterosaur in
the way.'

'Ask her to move,' grinned
Tom.

'*You* ask her!'
As if she had heard, the
mother quetzy
waddled

to the
cliff edge,
folded its wings and
raised its head, gazing out to sea.

'Look at the three bony crests over there,' whispered Jamie. 'Those are the babies. The mother must be guarding them in their nest.'

The baby quetzies were sitting in a hollow a few metres away.

'But where's Wanna?' Tom grabbed Jamie's arm. 'What if we're too late and they've already had him for dinner?'

*Grunk, grunk!*

A cone-shaped leathery hat with two brown eyes under it appeared over the edge of the nest.

'There he is!' exclaimed Tom.

'He's OK,' breathed Jamie in relief. 'But what's he wearing?'

'It's one of the quetzy eggshells,' Tom giggled. He stuck a hand out of the bush. 'Here, Wanna,' he beckoned.

'Come on, Wanna,' Jamie tried to coax him.

But Wanna just stared at them. He

seemed comfortable with his new friends.

'How do we lure him out?' said Tom.

Jamie rummaged in his backpack. 'I'll offer him a gingko. That should bring

him running.'

Trying to keep out of sight of the mother, Jamie crawled towards the nest. He had reached the edge when she spotted him.

*AAARK!*

Jamie ducked as the huge wing nearly caught him. He darted back to the bushes and Tom pulled him between the leaves and out of sight.

The gingko was squashed in his hand.

'It's just like on the documentaries,' said Tom. 'The mother is protecting her young and that makes her very dangerous.'

'One whack and I'd have been over the edge,' puffed Jamie. 'Now what?'

Tom didn't answer. He was looking up. Another quetzy was circling the nest.

'That one's even bigger than this one,' he said. 'It could be the dad.'

## *AARK, AAARK!*

The male quetzy landed next to the nest. His cry was deep and rumbling. The babies greeted him with screeches and squeals. Their heads bobbed and they eagerly opened their beaks. Wanna sat looking puzzled under his leathery hat. The dad bent his head down in a sudden motion and opened his mouth wide—right over Wanna's head. The boys heard a strange gurgling noise from his throat.

'He's going to eat him!' Jamie gasped. 'We've got to do something.'

But the male quetzy moved his head away from Wanna and over one

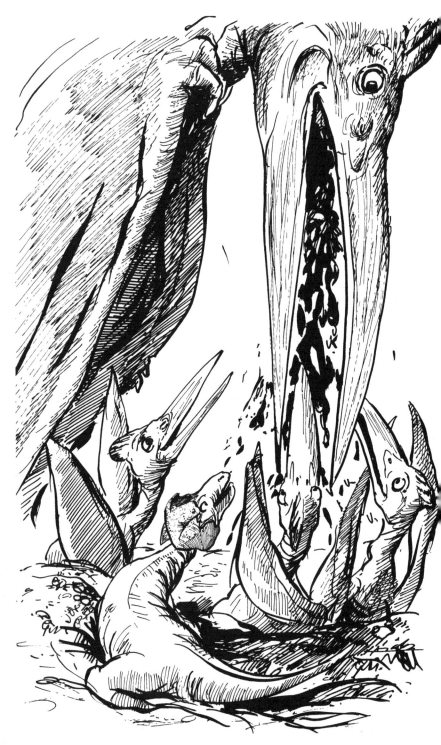

of his babies. He made the strange gurgling sound again and suddenly was sick into the baby quetzy's open beak. The little chick gulped hungrily. Then the dad bent to the next chick and puked again. The chick opened its mouth, caught the goo and gulped hungrily.

'Gross!' said Jamie.

'It's just like birds feeding their young,' said Tom. 'They mash down the food in their own throats and then bring it back up for them. And it's Wanna's turn now.'

The father gurgled again and all at once Wanna and his eggshell hat

were covered in steaming yellow goo.
Wanna looked surprised.

   Jamie laughed. 'They think he's
one of their chicks!'

CHAPTER 5

Wanna shook his head, splattering yellow goo everywhere. His eggshell hat went flying. Then he clambered out of the nest and began to sniff and scuff at the ground.

'That's our Wanna,' whispered Tom. 'He never sits still for long. He's too nosy.'

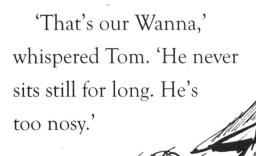

'I'd get out if a dinosaur was sick on my head,' said Jamie.

Tom craned round the bush. 'Wanna,' he called softly. 'Here, boy.'

*AAARK!*

The mother quetzy had seen Wanna. Wriggling her wings irritably, she scuttled round the nest and nudged him back with her beak.

When the
father had
finished feeding all
the chicks, he took
off and soared away.

'This is our best
chance to get Wanna,'
said Jamie. 'I'd rather
face one fierce quetzy
than two.'

'Agreed,' Tom
nodded.

The chicks began
to squawk excitedly
as the mother
picked one of

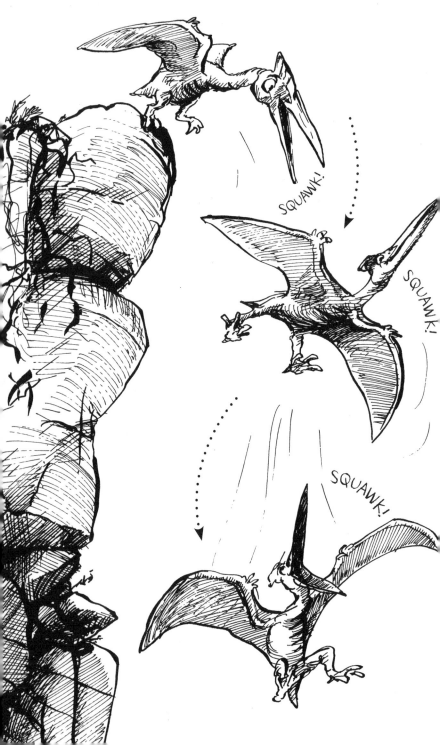

them up in her beak and plonked it down at the cliff edge.

'What's she doing?' Jamie gasped. 'The baby's going to fall off again.'

The little quetzy teetered on the edge for a moment and suddenly leapt off. They just had time to see it flapping its wings frantically before it plummeted out of sight.

The mother didn't seem to mind. She nudged another chick out of the nest and pushed it to the drop. This one flapped its wings and actually flew for a few seconds before it plunged down. They could hear its happy squawks as it fell.

'Of course,' said Jamie. 'It's Quetzy Flying School. The mum's teaching them how to fly.'

'And the cliffs are a perfect launching site,' said Tom. 'Plenty of height.'

The third baby waddled to the edge, opened its wings wide and vanished from sight. The boys heard a squeal of triumph and the little quetzy reappeared, flapping its wings and squawking at its mother. The mum squawked back encouragingly. Then the baby flew in a large circle and headed off out to sea.

'Perhaps the mother will go off

after them and we can rescue
Wanna,' said Tom hopefully.

But now the mother quetzy was
nudging Wanna towards the edge.

Jamie looked from Wanna to the
cliff top. 'She wants him to fly too!'

'Uh oh,' Tom said. 'We've got to
save him!'

They darted out from their hiding
place. Wanna was squatting on the
edge of the cliff. He grunked and
flapped his front legs as if he had
been watching the others.

*AARK!* The mother quetzy was
getting impatient. She prodded
Wanna and he nearly fell off the cliff.

Suddenly Jamie knew what to do.

'Grab him!' he yelled to Tom.
'We'll all jump down and aim for the
ledge below. It's our only chance.'

Dodging under the mother
quetzy's wings, the boys charged at
Wanna, seized him round the middle
and leapt off the cliff.

*Crunch!*

They landed in a heap in the bouncy creepers. One of the babies was there and it squealed with delight when it saw Wanna appear in front

of it. The boys gave each
other a high five.

'We made it!'

# AAARK!

'It's the mum,' said
Jamie urgently, looking up.
The quetzy was peering
over the edge of the cliff.
She poked her long beak
down and the boys had
to roll out of the way.
She opened her wings
and took to the air.

'We'd better get out of here before she circles round to rescue her chick—and Wanna. But how are we going to get him to the beach?'

'Perhaps we can make a rope out of the creepers,' suggested Tom. 'Then we can lower him.'

'It would work as long as we tie good knots,' said Jamie.

*Grunk, grunk!*

They turned to see Wanna clambering to the far end of the ledge and disappearing from view.

'Wait, Wanna,' cried Tom, scrambling across to see where he'd gone. 'You'll fall!'

But to his surprise Wanna was
trotting happily across the cliff
face. He'd found a little

trail that wound right down to the sand. The boys followed, placing each foot carefully on the narrow path.

'This is easier than the climb up,' said Tom.

'But not as exciting,' replied Jamie.

Swoosh! The mother quetzy swooped up past them, claws outstretched.

'She's come for her baby,' said Tom. 'I hope.'

The quetzy glided gracefully to the ledge and soon had her chick in her grasp. She made a wide, slow

circle over the beach. The boys held their breath.

Was she coming for Wanna now?

But after an anxious moment she rose to the cliff top and disappeared.

As soon as the boys stepped onto the sand, Wanna bounded up and head butted them affectionately.

'Let's get you home, boy,' said Tom. 'Before your new mother comes looking for you.'

They set off back into the jungle, Wanna running alongside them, grunking happily.

As they followed the river back to Wanna's cave, Jamie stopped and

wrinkled his nose. 'What's that smell?'

'It's Wanna,' Tom laughed. 'He's still covered in quetzy puke.'

'Yuck!' Jamie held his nose. 'Someone needs a bath.'

He waded into the shallows and held out a gingko. Wanna bounded into the river.

'Great,' said Tom, jumping in to join them. 'We can give him a shower.'

He cupped his hands in the water and splashed Wanna all over.

Then Wanna turned and thumped the surface with his tail. Jamie and Tom got soaked.

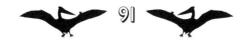

'Thanks, Wanna,' said Tom. 'At least that gross yellow puke has gone.'

Finally, they climbed out of the shallows and made their way up the hill to Wanna's cave.

*Grunk.*

Wanna ran straight to his nest and curled up.

'You've got the right nest this time,' grinned Jamie. He took the last gingkoes out of his bag and put them by Wanna's side. 'See you soon, little friend.'

They put their feet in the dinosaur footprints and walked backwards towards the cave wall into the smugglers' cave. They hurried out of the cave and down the headland, running all the way along the beach to the path that led up Sealight Head. After waiting a little while for

the sun to dry out their clothes, they raced up the steps, two at a time, and burst through the door of the lighthouse.

'We must have been away ages,' gasped Jamie. 'Dad's done so much.'

They gazed at the breathtaking displays of dinosaur models and fossils all around the room.

'Awesome!' Tom pointed at a huge ammonite. 'It's as big as a tyre.'

Jamie wandered round, taking it all in. 'The triceratops skull looks great up on the wall.'

His dad came in at that moment, laden with books.

'Hello there, boys,' he called. 'Found anything out about the quetzy nest?'

The boys went over to the model Cretaceous landscape. 'We think it would have nested here on the cliff top,' said Jamie. 'There's lots of room for those huge wings and it's a perfect take-off point.'

'The babies could learn to fly from there,' added Tom eagerly. 'It's very high and there'd be uplift from the wind coming off the ocean.'

'Good thinking, boys,' said Jamie's dad. He placed the quetzalcoatlus carefully down on the cliff top.

'They'd be able to skim down over the sea and catch their dinner.'

Jamie looked at the quetzalcoatlus model, its wings outstretched ready for flight. He winked at Tom.

'That's not all they catch,' he whispered.

DINOSAUR WORLD

– – – – BOYS' ROUTE

Jungle

Misty
Lagoon

White
Ocean

98

Far Away Mountains

Crashing
Rock
Falls

Great
Plains

Fang
Rock

Gingko
Hill

# GLOSSARY

**Baculite** (back-you-lite) – an extinct sea creature that swam upside down with its head sticking out from the bottom of its long thin shell. Because baculite fossils are fragile, fossil hunters rarely find a fossilized baculite shell intact.

**Elasmosaurus** (ee-laz-mow-sor-us) – a long-necked prehistoric sea creature with a small head, sharp teeth, and four flippers. Elasmosaurus may have stretched 14 metres long, with its neck making up half of its total length.

**Gingko** (gink-oh) – a tree native to China called a 'living fossil' because fossils of it have been found dating back millions of years, yet they are still around today. Also known as the stink bomb tree because of its smelly apricot-like fruit.

**Platecarpus** (plat-ee-carp-us) – an extinct sharp-toothed lizard with a long, flat tail and flippers which may have swum like a snake in prehistoric waters.

100

**Pterosaur** (ter-oh-sor) – a prehistoric flying reptile. Its wings were leathery and light and some of these 'winged lizards' had fur on their bodies and bony crests on their heads.

**Quetzalcoatlus** (ket-sal-kow-at-lus) – one of the largest flying animals ever. Named after the Aztec feathered serpent god Quetzalcoatl, this prehistoric bird had a long neck, toothless jaw, and a long bony crest on top of its head. Its clawed wings could span up to 12 metres across.

**Wannanosaurus** (wah-nan-oh-sor-us) – a dinosaur that only ate plants and used its hard, flat skull to defend itself. Named after the place it was discovered: Wannano in China.

# If you blink
# you'll miss me . . .
## and I'm coming next!

Turn the page

to read the

first chapter of the

next adventure in the

# Dinosaur Cove™

series:

Catching the
Speedy Thief

Jamie Morgan pulled a rainbow-
coloured metal fish out of his
grandad's tackle box and held it up
for his friend Tom Clay to see. 'This
fish has feathers!' A cluster of tiny

sea bass spinner

crab line

pink and orange feathers sprouted out from where the tail should be.

'Different baits catch different beasts,' Jamie's grandad said with a grin, holding out his hand for the feathery fish. 'This spinner is great for catching sea bass. Now, let's see. What else will I need today?' He tipped a tangle of weights, spinners, and fishing line onto the kitchen floor of the old lighthouse.

'What's this?' Jamie picked up an H-shaped piece of orange plastic with string wrapped around it and a couple of heavy lead weights dangling from it.

'Haven't you seen one before?' Tom said in amazement. 'It's a crab line.'

Jamie shook his head. 'How can this catch crabs?'

'It's easy,' Tom said. 'You tie a bit of bacon rind on the end and throw it in. The crabs grab the bacon and you grab the crabs!'

'Cool!' said Jamie. 'I'd like to try that.'

'The best place for crabbing is
Sealight Head at high tide,' Grandad
said, as he crammed everything but
the crab line back in his tackle box.
'But high tide isn't until later this
afternoon. I'll meet you there, if
you like, after I've caught some
sea bass for dinner.'

'OK, Grandad,' Jamie
said as the old man

finished packing his tackle box. 'We'll wait until then.'

'We don't have to wait,' Tom whispered to Jamie. 'We could go crabbing in Misty Lagoon in Dino World right now.'

Dino World was Jamie and Tom's secret—even Grandad didn't know that they'd found a world where real live dinosaurs lived.

'Great idea!' Jamie winked at Tom. 'We'll meet you near Sealight Head later, Grandad.'

'Don't forget the bait and mop bucket to put the crabs in,' Grandad told them. He pulled on his fishing boots. 'And I've put two cheese and pickle sandwiches in the fridge for you.' He headed for the door. 'Have fun!'

'We will,' Tom said with a smile. The minute Grandad was out of the door Tom grabbed the handle of the mop bucket. 'Got your Fossil Finder, Jamie?'

'Already in my backpack.' Jamie grinned as he wrapped two cheese and pickle sandwiches in shiny tinfoil and made a separate package for the bacon. He stuffed them in his

backpack along with the
crab line. 'Let's go!'

The boys clattered down
the stairs of the lighthouse
and dashed through the
dinosaur exhibits on the
ground floor. Jamie's dad
was busy fixing a label to

the wall next to the triceratops skull.

'How's the museum going, Mr Morgan?' Tom asked.

'Great, thanks,' said Jamie's dad. 'The Grand Opening is only a few days away.'

'See ya, Dad!' Jamie called, hurrying past the Late Cretaceous model and the t-rex display. 'We're going crabbing.'

The boys scrambled down the rocky path from the lighthouse and ran along the beach onto the trail that led up Smuggler's Point. They bent double to catch their breath, and then clambered up the boulders to the smugglers' cave and squeezed through the gap at the back into the secret chamber.

'This is my favourite place in the whole world!' Jamie's heart began to pound as soon as he placed his feet into the fossilized dinosaur footprints on the cave floor.

'One . . . two . . . three . . . ' He counted each step. 'Keep close behind me, Tom.'

'You bet.' Tom's voice sounded excited. 'I wonder what we're going to find this time.'

'Four . . . ' A crack of light appeared in the cave wall in front of him.

'Five!' The ground squelched beneath Jamie's feet and he stood blinking in the  bright sunshine and breathing in the familiar warm wet-leaf smell of Dino World.

A second later,
Jamie and Tom were
standing on Gingko Hill,
and a rough, slobbery tongue
was licking Jamie's hand.

'Ready for another adventure,
Wanna?' Jamie asked their little
dinosaur friend.

Jamie picked a stinky gingko fruit and held it out to the wannanosaurus.

Wanna took it gently, then greedily gobbled it up, wagging his tail and grunking as smelly gingko juice dribbled down his chin.

'It's almost like he was waiting for us,' Tom said with a laugh.

With Tom and Wanna close behind, Jamie strode through the trees to a curtain of creepers at the edge of Gingko Hill. As he pushed the creepers aside, excitement fizzed like soda in his stomach.

Beneath them lay the steamy emerald-green jungle. The air throbbed with the whirring and buzzing of insects, and the jungle rang with the strange calls of the weird and wonderful creatures that only lived in Dino World.

'This has got to be the best place for adventures in the whole wide world!' Jamie announced with a huge grin on his face.

'In the whole solar system!' Tom cheered.

'In the whole universe!' Jamie exclaimed.

Wanna grunked his agreement.

'Come on!' Jamie said. 'Let's see what we can catch in Misty Lagoon. We've only got until the tide comes in.'

The three friends clambered down the steep hillside into the dense jungle.

'We can follow the stream,' Jamie said, jumping into the shallow water that trickled and gurgled its way to the lagoon.

They splashed along the stream bed.

'That's where we met the t-rex,' Tom said, pointing to a jumble of huge rounded rocks.

'I'll never forget those fangs.' Jamie shuddered. 'I hope he's not around today.'

'Me too,' said Tom, looking round nervously. 'Let's get a move on.'

They ran until they burst out of the jungle onto the palm-fringed sandy beach of the sparkling blue lagoon.

Jamie shaded his eyes with his hand and gazed round the shore.

'Which would be the best spot to find prehistoric crabs?'

'We need deep water for crabbing,' Tom told him. 'It's no use wading into the shallows.'

'How about over there?' Jamie pointed to an outcrop of fern-covered rocks on the north-east shore. A stone ledge stuck out of the ferns like a wide diving board, hanging over the deep, blue water.

'Perfect!' Tom declared.

Join Jamie and Tom
in **Dino World**
with the

# Dinosaur Cove™

# CRETACEOUS
# SURVIVAL GUIDE

Turn the page for a taster
of all the awesome
things to do . . .

# Create!

## MAKE YOUR OWN EDIBLE DINO POO!

### YOU WILL NEED:

- 100g plain chocolate
- 50g margarine
- 2 tablespoons golden syrup
- 150g plain digestive biscuits

**1** Put the biscuits in a large freezer bag and tie the bag shut. Using a rolling pin, bash the biscuits into crumbs.

**2** Break up the chocolate into pieces and put them in a saucepan. Heat the pan on a low temperature until the chocolate has melted.

Don't forget to ask a grown-up to help melt the chocolate!

**3** Stir the margarine and syrup into the melted chocolate.

**4** Take the saucepan off the heat. Pour the biscuit crumbs into the chocolate mixture and stir together.

36 37

# Play!

WHICH CRETACEOUS DINO ARE YOU?

START
Do you walk on two legs or four legs?

Two legs

Four legs

Super speedy or supremely strong?

Super speedy or supremely strong?

Speedy

Strong

Biscuits

Speedy

Up high or down low?

Protected by horns or bony armour?

Carnivore or herbivore?

Down low

Up high

Horns

Bony armour

Hunt on land or in the air?

Carnivore

Herbivore

Land

Air

T-Rex   Quetzalcoatlus   Velociraptor   Wannanosaurus

Bagaceratops   Edmontosaurus   Triceratops   Ankylosaurus

Join Jamie and Tom
in **Dino World**
with the

# Dinosaur Cove™

## CRETACEOUS SURVIVAL GUIDE

Turn the page for a taster
of all the **awesome**
things to do . . .

# Create!

## MAKE YOUR OWN EDIBLE DINO POO!

### YOU WILL NEED:

- 100g plain chocolate
- 50g margarine
- 2 tablespoons golden syrup
- 150g plain digestive biscuits

**1** Put the biscuits in a large freezer bag and tie the bag shut. Using a rolling pin, bash the biscuits into crumbs.

**2** Break up the chocolate into pieces and put them in a saucepan. Heat the pan on a low temperature until the chocolate has melted.

Don't forget to ask a grown-up to help melt the chocolate!

**3** Stir the margarine and syrup into the melted chocolate.

**4** Take the saucepan off the heat. Pour the biscuit crumbs into the chocolate mixture and stir together.

36  37

# Play!

## WHICH CRETACEOUS DINO ARE YOU?

**START**
Do you walk on two legs or four legs?

Two legs — Super speedy or supremely strong?

Speedy — Hunt on land or in the air?

Strong — Carnivore or herbivore?

Land — T-Rex
Air — Quetzalcoatlus
Carnivore — Velociraptor
Herbivore — Wannanosaurus

Four legs — Super speedy or supremely strong?

Speedy — Up high or down low?

Down low — Bagaceratops
Up high — Edmontosaurus

Strong — Protected by horns or bony armour?

Horns — Triceratops
Bony armour — Ankylosaurus